THE PRAYER of JESUS

FOR YOU

THE PRAYER OF JESUS FOR YOU

Text copyright © 2002 Hank Hanegraaff. Based on *The Prayer of Jesus* by Hank Hanegraaff.

Published in Nashville, Tennessee, by Tommy Nelson®, a Division of Thomas Nelson, Inc.

Scripture quotations noted (NIV) are from the *Holy Bible,* New International Version; © 1973, 1978, 1984, International Bible Society. Used by permission of Zondervan Bible Publishers. Scripture quotations noted (ICB) are from the *International Children's Bible®, New Century Version®;* © 1986, 1989, 1999 by Tommy Nelson®, a Division of Thomas Nelson, Inc., Nashvllle, Tennessee, 37214. Used by permission.

Library of Congress Control Number: 2002104919

ISBN: 1-4003-0112-2

Printed in the United States of America

02 03 04 05 06 WRZ 5 4 3 2 1

30 DAYS 30 WAYS
CLOSER TO GOD

THE
PRaYeR
of JeSuS
FOr YOU

HANK HANEGRAAFF

adaptation by Monica Hall
from *The Prayer of Jesus*

Tommy nelson™
A Division of Thomas Nelson, Inc.
www.tommynelson.com
www.ThomasNelson.com

CONTENTS

Day 1   "Lord, Teach Us *Now* to Pray"   1

Day 2   The Secret   4

Day 3   Prayer Is Its Own Reward   7

Day 4   God Always Responds   10

Day 5   Eternal Rewards   13

Day 6   Your Father Knows   16

Day 7   Principles of Prayer   19

Day 8   So Why Ask?   22

Day 9   Building Our Relationship with God   25

Day 10   "Our Father in Heaven . . ."   28

Day 11   "Hallowed Be Your Name . . ."   31

Day 12   "Your Kingdom Come . . ."   34

Day 13   "Your Will Be Done . . ."   37

Day 14   "On Earth As It Is in Heaven . . ."   40

Day 15   Bringing Our Requests   43

Day 16 "Give Us Today Our Daily Bread . . ." 46

Day 17 "Daily Bread" Is *More* Than Just Something to Eat 49

Day 18 "Forgive Us Our Debts . . ." 52

Day 19 ". . . As We Also Have Forgiven Our Debtors" 55

Day 20 The Compassion Award 58

Day 21 "And Lead Us Not into Temptation . . ." 61

Day 22 "But Deliver Us from the Evil One" 64

Day 23 Putting On Our Armor 67

Day 24 Into the Deep 70

Day 25 Praying "Backward" 73

Day 26 "The Sounds of Silence" 76

Day 27 The Secret Place 79

Day 28 The Chance of a Lifetime! 82

Day 29 "For Yours Is the Kingdom . . ." 85

Day 30 "Amen." 88

Prayer Tracker 91

Your hands are sweaty.
Your face is hot.
Your knees are shaking.

And you're not sure you can even *stand* . . . never mind *walk* to the front of the room.

GULP! You—yes, *you!*—have to make a speech!

Everyone is expecting you to say something *wonderful* . . . and you're not even sure you can say *anything* at all. It's not that you don't want to do well. It's just that you can't seem to find the words.

Ever feel that way? Okay, maybe nothing quite so . . . *dramatic.* But most all of us hit times when putting our thoughts into words brings on the butterflies.

Maybe it's a class report . . . or leading your youth group devotional . . . or accepting an award (I didn't say you were untalented, just uncomfortable) that makes you **"clutch up"** inside.

Or maybe . . . just *maybe* . . . it's the thought of talking to *God* that brings out your "shy" side?

Do you have trouble getting started? Run out of things to say? Feel that there's something *missing* in your prayers? Wish you could feel *closer* to God?

Now, what if . . . someone could . . .

Show you how to pray the way God wants you to **pray** . . .

Bring prayer *alive* for you . . .

Give you a passion for praying?!

Wouldn't you jump at the chance? Well, so did the disciples!

Boy, did they jump . . .

DAY 1

"Lord, Teach Us *Now* to Pray"

> *One day Jesus was praying in a certain*
> *place. When he finished, one of his disciples*
> *said to him, "Lord, teach us to pray, just as*
> *John taught his disciples."*
>
> — LUKE 11:1 (NIV)

Lord, teach us to pray." It doesn't sound like an unusual request. But in the Greek language of Luke 11:1, the tone is a bit more urgent—as if that eager disciple blurts out, "Lord, teach us *now* to pray." Why the big rush? What made it so important that Jesus teach them to pray *right now?!*

Surely the disciples already knew all kinds of prayers. The Bible is full of them. Prayers of praise. Prayers of "asking." Even prayers that simply say "thank you" (though *those* tend to get a little dusty from lack of use). But nothing that brought the look of peace Jesus wore when *he* returned from prayer.

The disciples might not have known exactly *what* it was, but they knew they wanted it.

And they wanted it now!

▰▰ THERE'S NOTHING LIKE AN EAGER AUDIENCE

I don't know about you, but I can practically see a big grin spreading across Jesus' face when he heard that question. What teacher doesn't live for the moment when a student *asks to learn?*

Jesus knew if the disciples were to learn how to really talk to God, they needed more than just another *example* of prayer; they needed to understand the *principles* of prayer.

1

So Jesus gave them not just *a* prayer, but the *pattern* for all prayer. And the disciples learned it well. Within just a few short years, they had turned their world upside down!

The Prayer of Jesus made a difference in the disciples' lives, and it can do the same for you . . . so keep reading . . . make the journey . . . learn the secret.

■■■■■ CAUSE FOR EXCITEMENT

Now, maybe it's never occurred to you that there *is* a "secret"—something *more* to prayer than you know about. Something so *special* that it can change your life . . . *and* your relationship with God!

But even if you've never thought about it at all, I am pretty sure you *do* know exactly how those disciples felt. After all, they were students—just like you—with an opportunity to learn something wonderful . . . from a master teacher. Wouldn't that make *you* pretty eager, even excited?

■■■■■ SEIZING THE MOMENT

Maybe you've always dreamed of moving the soccer ball down the field with nimble-footed, catch-me-if-you-can skill. Then, one day . . . one *unbelievable* day . . . your all-time favorite soccer hero drops by your team practice. (It *could* happen.) You're not going to let the chance to ask for a tip . . . or ten . . . get away, are you?

Or maybe it's dance you love. And a famous ballerina is teaching a one-day master class in your town. *Who's* up, dressed, and out the door—ballet slippers in hand—at 5:00 A.M.?!

Or fill in *your* favorite "If only I could. . . ." Then imagine the world's greatest master of that art is standing right in front of you.

See . . . you *do* know all about "eager" and "urgent." And those are just talents and skills of *this* world. But what if—like the disciples—you were face-to-face with the opportunity to grow closer to *God* than you ever dared dream?!

Guess what? *You are.* Make the journey!

When opportunity knocks, do you say, "Leave a message; I'll get back to you"? Or do you fling the door wide open and say, "Come on in!"? Kind of a no-brainer, right?

Well, you're looking at the opportunity of a lifetime right now . . . a chance to invite God into your life . . . and "connect" one-on-one with God in prayer!

All you have to do is open the door . . . and begin . . . right from where you are—right now—in your prayer life.

→ **When I pray, these are the things I usually talk about:**

→ **I wonder what would happen if I**

→ **These are the times especially when I wish I felt closer to God:**

WaNna wriTe moRe? UsE tHe PraYer TracKer tHat staRts On pAge 91 tO tRacK yOur prayEr prAisEs aNd reQueSts.

3

 D1

DAY 2

The Secret

> But when you pray, go into your room,
> close the door and pray to your Father,
> who is unseen. Then your Father, who
> sees what is done in secret, will reward you.
>
> — MATTHEW 6:6 (NIV)

Secrets. How we love them! And how we want to *know* them. There's nothing quite like feeling we're on the inside track . . . having the straight scoop on what makes things, and people, tick.

How *does* Michelle Kwan glide over the ice with such breathtaking grace to win six national and four world titles and two Olympic medals?

How does she perform with such brilliance? What's her *secret?!*

Ask her, and she might be amazed you think she even *has* a secret. Surely everyone *must* know it's what happens "offstage" that counts?!

For every four-minute program in the spotlight before cheering thousands, there are hundreds of *hours* of Michelle-alone-on-the-ice. Practicing. Working at it. Perfecting her art—not for the applause, but for the love of skating. When *nobody* is watching. In secret, you might say. Which, come to think of it, *is* the secret. Just as it is with prayer.

■■■■■ THE SECRET TO PRAYER IS SECRET PRAYER

Prayer is not a public performance; it is—or should be—"time alone" with God.

The goal of prayer isn't the roaring approval of the crowd, but the sweet silent approval of our Father in heaven.

Jesus knew the secret, and he shared it with us: ". . . when you pray, go into your room, close the door and pray to your Father. . . ." And he didn't just *tell* us; he showed us. He "often withdrew to lonely places and prayed" (Luke 5:16 NIV).

Jesus knew the secret to deep and true relationships is time alone together. He took that time with God. You can, too.

▮▮▮▮▮ JUST HANGING OUT

Relationships—friendships—are strange and wonderful things. No two are ever quite alike. Each has its own style, its own pace.

But there's *one* thing you'll find in *all* the really good ones; they're just so . . . comfortable. They're as natural as breathing.

Isn't it that way with you and *your* best friend? It's not so much *what* you do as it is doing it *together*. Well, sure, you both have other friends, too. And there are a lot of fun group things you enjoy, together *and* apart.

But when you really want to relax . . . just be yourself . . . there's nothing quite like hanging out with your best friend. Just being together. Doing nothing in particular.

Sometimes you're yakking away nonstop. Other times all it takes is just a glance—or a grin—to crack you both up, without a word spoken. You're "connected." On the same wavelength. In sync. And the more time you spend together, the stronger that connection grows.

▮▮▮▮▮ THE BEST FRIEND OF ALL

Now imagine connecting with God like that. Imagine feeling that comfortable—that no-questions-asked *welcome*—in *his* presence. Not asking for anything. Not "explaining" or making excuses about anything. Just being together with someone who knows you and loves you and accepts you in Christ just as you are. Just . . . hanging out. For the joy of it.

Can't quite picture it? Don't worry; God can. He's just waiting for *you* to "get the picture," too.

D²

How *do* you put yourself in the picture—create a wonderful relation-ship—with God? Well, you could start by taking a look at how you feel about—and deal with—friendship in general.

→ **I am a good friend because**

→ **I could be a *better* friend if I would**

→ **When I think about prayer as just "being together" with God, I**

DAY 3

Prayer Is Its Own Reward

"Test me in this," says the Lord . . .
"I will open the windows of heaven
for you. I will pour out more blessings
than you have room for."

— MALACHI 3:10 (ICB)

Ever taken a close look at the faces of star performers while they're doing what they do so well? Thanks to film and video closeups, you can practically "rub elbows" with all your sports and entertainment favorites.

But have you really *looked* at those faces . . . wondered what's going on *behind* them? *You* might be at a concert or competition, but *they* are somewhere else entirely. They are completely *inside* themselves . . . lost in the moment.

Sure, they want to perform brilliantly. And, yes, they love applause. But all that's for later. While they're "in the game," all that matters is the joy of *doing*.

THE PROCESS IS THE PRIZE

Applause fades away. Awards get misplaced. But the joy of throwing your heart into something you love fills you to the brim every time you do it!

It can be that way with prayer, too. *If* you look at prayer as Jesus did. He knew that prayer is not a secret formula to get things from God, or to impress other people. Just being with God—talking to him in prayer—*is* the reward.

7

Ever thought about prayer that way? Not everyone does. All too often we measure the "success" of our prayer lives by the size of our accomplishments and possessions, rather than our closeness with God. We look at outside things. God cares about what's *inside*.

FILLING THE EMPTY SPACE

There is an empty space inside each of us that only God can fill. Pascal, who was a thinker who flat "got it," described it as "a God-shaped vacuum." And you know what a vacuum *does:* It draws things in!

God wants to fill that space in our lives. But we have to invite him in. If we allow worldly things to slip in and fill God's place instead, we end up still feeling *empty*. Only God is the "perfect fit" for that space. And it's prayer that invites him in. Prayer itself *is* the gift. And gifts are meant to be enjoyed!

CELEBRATING YOUR GIFTS

Maybe God gave you a gift for music or art . . . or math. Maybe you run like a deer or swim like a fish. Or maybe *your* special gift is a glad heart . . . or a talent for making people smile.

Some of your gifts you might already know about. Others might stay hidden until later in life. But there's *one* gift you can absolutely . . . positively! . . . count on *all* the time: The gift of prayer. All you have to do is *use* it.

And here's the best part: Like any gift, the more you do use it, the better you get at it. And the better you get at it, the more joy it brings you! Not because of what other people think or say. Not for rewards or applause. But because of the way it makes you *feel* . . . inside.

Learn the Prayer of Jesus. Practice it every day. And taste the sweet joy of growing closer to the One who made you . . . and fills your life with *every* gift.

So here you are, looking at the lovely gift—and fantastic *opportunity*—called "prayer." It's yours for the taking. If you want it. If you're willing to *work* for it.

Kind of takes your breath away, doesn't it? In fact, it might be so much more than you ever expected that you're not quite sure *what* to do with it. That's okay. Sometimes the really great gifts do stop you in your tracks. Take your time. Regroup. Maybe rethink your old ideas about prayer.

→ **If someone had asked you to *define* prayer before now, what would you have said?**

→ **How would you answer that question *now?***

→ **How does looking at the idea of prayer in this new way make you feel?**

DAY 4

God Always Responds

I will pray to the Lord.
And he will answer me
from his holy mountain.
—PSALM 3:4 (ICB)

When we pray, God not only listens . . . he acts. Secret prayer is always rewarded by a *response* from God.

As we spend time with him in prayer, God hears what we say . . . and what we don't say. He knows what we want . . . and what we *need*. And his answer comes from a heart overflowing with love.

Of course, the response we get from God might not be the response we want. But it is always the *right* response. Joni Eareckson Tada found that out.

A JOURNEY BEGINS

Back in the 1960s, Joni was a lively teenager with a strong, athletic body that did everything she asked of it. Until the diving accident—when she hit the water horribly . . . disastrously . . . wrong.

When she woke up in the hospital, she was inside a body that no longer did *anything* she asked of it. Her neck was broken, and Joni would spend the rest of her life in a wheelchair.

During the long weeks and months that followed, she'd listen for hours as her friends read her stories from the Scriptures. One of her favorites was the story of a man who had been an invalid for thirty-eight years—until the day he was healed by Jesus at the Pool of Bethesda.

Joni began picturing herself lying by that pool. And for hours on end she'd plead with God for a miraculous healing. But God, it seemed, wasn't going to answer that particular prayer.

But Joni never gave up on God. She never stopped talking to him. And as she grew closer to God, year by year, the "asking" became less and less important. Just being *with* God filled her life—and overflowed into her inspirational books that would touch multitudes of *other* lives.

THINGS AREN'T ALWAYS WHAT THEY SEEM

Thirty years later—sitting in her wheelchair by the Pool of Bethesda—Joni was filled with joy . . . as the truth struck her. God had given her *more* than she'd asked for!

He hadn't healed her body; he had *opened* her heart . . . made her life ever richer and deeper through prayer . . . and taught her spirit to fly farther and higher than legs could ever have carried her.

Ever have that happen to you . . . ask for one thing, and get something else instead? Maybe it was a coach who was a real "nut" on practicing the fundamentals. Or an English teacher who was positively *fixated* on the idea of perfect grammar.

You, of course, just wanted to get to the *fun* part: Playing like a champion. Writing that brilliant story. That's what you wanted. But what you *needed* was exactly what you got . . . so that when your "moment" arrived, you were ready.

GOD ALWAYS KNOWS WHAT HE'S DOING

It's that way with prayer, too. You might wonder if God hears you at all. Or *why* he never seems to answer your prayers.

And while you're busy stewing about all that, *God* is busy filling your life with the things he knows you need. So you'll have them . . . when your "moment" arrives.

D4

Of course, nothing might have happened in your life—so far—as dramatic as what happened for Joni Eareckson Tada. (Though with God's hand at work, you can never be absolutely sure.) And maybe playing sports . . . or writing a story . . . is the very last thing *you'd* ever do. So let's look at this whole idea of what you ask for and what you get from *your* point of view.

→ **How did God answer one of your prayers in an unexpected way?**

OLD GIRLFRIEND, PRAYED TO GET BACK TOGETHER,
BUT GOD ANSWERED THE PRAYER DIFFERENTLY.
SOON AFTER I MET MY WIFE.

→ **What have you asked God for lately?**

BETTER Communication

→ **Knowing what you know *now*, how *might* God choose to answer that prayer?**

MATH. 8:23

DAY 5

Eternal Rewards

Before the mountains were born
or you brought forth the earth
and the world, from everlasting
to everlasting you are God.
> —PSALM 90:2 (NIV)

Eternity: Forever. Endless. From everlasting to everlasting. *Beyond* the beyond . . .

Kind of makes you dizzy to think about it, doesn't it? How can we possibly wrap our minds around an idea as enormous as *eternity?* Fortunately, we don't have to. Because all of eternity fits very neatly inside *God's* mind. And we can trust him to get it right. All *we* have to think about—and prepare for—is our place in it.

■■■■ "TREASURES IN HEAVEN"

That's the other gift in mastering the art of prayer. It prepares us for eternity. And there's nothing we will ever do that is more important!

Jesus made that perfectly clear when he warned his followers not to store up "treasures on earth, where moth and rust destroy, and where thieves break in and steal" (Matthew 6:19 NIV). Instead, he said, store up "treasures in heaven." Prayer helps us do that.

As we "stretch" our spirits through daily prayer, we grow in other ways, too. Our ability to love expands. We care more about the needs of others. We learn to accept responsibility with joy and to serve with love. We become better people!

Best of all—just as mastering an instrument increases our enjoyment of music—mastering prayer prepares us to *enjoy* eternity. Just as God wants us to.

■■■■ THE FINE ART OF GOING THE DISTANCE

Have you heard the story about the teen who was supposed to meet a friend in front of Carnegie Hall? But New York City is big, and even something as impressive as one of the world's great concert halls proved impossible to find.

Clearly, he needed help.

"Pardon me, sir," he asked a passerby, "how can I get to Carnegie Hall?"

The man—a famous violinist on his way to *perform* there—looked at him, and smiled. "Practice, my boy," he answered. "Practice!"

Okay, it probably never really happened. But the story does make the point: To perform brilliantly takes work!

Not really a surprise, is it? You figured out quite awhile ago that it takes time—and effort—to master just about anything.

You didn't just stand up and walk one day, did you? Or how about that first solo bike ride?!

Of course, you might have zipped through long division. But then along came history or science, and there you were again, digging in. Because it's patience and perseverance and *work* that bring goals within reach.

■■■■ REACHING FOR ETERNITY

Through prayer you're reaching for the most wonderful goal of all: A personal relationship with God *now* . . . and forever.

Yes, like any skill, there's work involved in mastering prayer. But it's work filled with joy. Because all the time you're learning the basics, practicing and polishing your skills, you are doing it *with God!* And *he's* there with you every step of the way.

Still having trouble with the whole idea of eternity? Try this. Picture the number 8. Now tip it over onto its side. You're looking at the symbol for eternity. No beginning. No end. Everything connects to everything else in one unbroken line. "Now" and "then" are just different points on the same line. Which means that everything you do *now* touches everything else! Kinda makes you think, doesn't it?

→ **When I think about eternity, I see**

→ **If I *am* getting ready for eternity right now, I'd better**

MAKE SURE I AM IN DAILY PRAYER & DEVOTION AND BECOMING CLOSER TO CHRIST.

→ **Here are some *practical* ways I can make prayer part of my life every day:**

DURING BREAKFAST, BEFORE I GO TO BED BEFORE YOU EAT AND EVEN AT SCHOOL OR WHILE DRIVING ANYWHERE.

D5

DAY 6

Your Father Knows

"And when you pray, do not keep on babbling like pagans, for they think they will be heard because of their many words. Do not be like them, for your Father knows what you need before you ask him."
— MATTHEW 6:7–8 (NIV)

If there's one thing people are good at, it's talking. We can go on for hours, often—very often—saying nothing important at all.

Jesus knew that. He also knew about one of our *other* favorite things: shortcuts. We *love* quick and easy! (Never mind that a lot of shortcuts don't work.)

Yes, Jesus knew how much we love the sound of our own voices . . . *and* getting what we want the easy way. And he wanted to make sure neither mistake would happen with the perfect prayer he was about to teach the disciples. It was neither a formula to be "recited" nor a shortcut to getting things from God.

A LITTLE FRIENDLY ADVICE

Jesus warned the disciples that words *alone* are not enough. And he warned them about asking over and over for earthly things, because "your Father knows what you need *before* you ask him" (Matthew 6:8 NIV).

What?! (Can't you practically *see* their puzzled looks?) *If God already knows what we want, why bother praying at all?!*

It's a trap a lot of people fall into—thinking that prayer is only about "asking" and "getting." Jesus was about to teach them—and us—the *true* purpose of prayer: Communicating with God. And just being with him!

■■■■ PLANTING THE SEED . . . TENDING THE GARDEN

We don't have to make a lot of noise to get God's attention; we already have it. And just because God knows our hopes and fears and needs doesn't mean he doesn't want us to talk them over with him.

In fact, he *longs* for communication with us. Because that's how relationships grow. And there *are* no shortcuts for that.

You probably know a little bit about shortcuts yourself, right? You know . . . stuffing your dirty clothes under the bed instead of the laundry hamper . . . borrowing a friend's homework instead of doing your own . . . falling into bed without brushing your teeth . . . ? They might even work, for a while. Until . . . you're out of clean clothes . . . you flunk math . . . you get a cavity. The truth is, when you leave out your *best* effort, you're cheating more than just . . . you! You're cheating God, and others too.

■■■■ ARE YOU CHEATING YOURSELF, TOO?

Here's a thought: What if you're cheating yourself when it comes to prayer?!

If you're just mumbling some memorized words, listing your requests and thinking, *There . . . that's done,* you are! Because, with prayer, you *could* be building a wonderful *relationship* with God . . . who surely deserves the very best you have to offer.

But if God already knows what's in my mind and heart, what am I going to talk about?!

How about everything *in* your mind and heart! God is always ready to listen . . . *whatever* you have to say. Because that's how friendships grow. It's spending time together that matters. God wants that. With *you.*

D6

If you've never thought of prayer as a *conversation* with God, now would be a good time to take a look at that idea. Why not start by thinking about how you talk with friends . . . and how you usually talk with God?

→ **My friends and I usually talk about**

→ **When I talk with God, I usually say**

→ **Some things I'd really *like* to talk to God about but never have:**

DAY 7

Principles of Prayer

The Lord is close to everyone
who prays to him,
to all who truly pray to him.

—PSALM 145:18 (ICB)

Prayer is the "link" that connects us to our Father in heaven. And the more we pray—*truly* pray—the stronger and more beautiful our relationship grows.

How can we be sure that our prayers are everything they *could* be? Jesus showed us the way—when he taught the disciples not just *a* prayer, but the *principles* of prayer. Learn those principles, use them in their proper order, and the secret of prayer is yours.

To help you remember the priorities of prayer, here's a handy little reminder. . . .

▄▄▄▄▄ JUST THE F-A-C-T-S

Just remember **F**aith, **A**doration, **C**onfession, **T**hanksgiving, **S**upplication, and you've got the principles of prayer in a nutshell.

Faith. Faith is only as strong as the object in which we place it. It is *what* we believe—and *who* we believe in—that makes belief possible. The secret is not in the words we say, but in coming to know the One to whom we say them. And there's no better way to get to know God than through Jesus and Scripture.

Adoration. Faith in God just naturally leads to adoration. Prayer *without* adoration is like a body without a soul. It is not only incomplete; it just

D7

doesn't work! Through adoration we tell God how much we love and long for him. And as we think of the wonder of God, we just naturally want to praise and worship him.

Need inspiration? The Scriptures—especially the Psalms—are overflowing with wonderful words of adoration.

Confession. Yes, we *are* redeemed by the person and work of Jesus. But that doesn't mean we can't—and don't—sin. When we do, we need to admit it and tell God we're sorry.

Without confession, our conversation with God is missing something essential to any relationship: Truth. By saying, "I was wrong; I'm sorry; please forgive me," we put ourselves right with God again.

Thanksgiving. Nothing is more basic to prayer than thanksgiving. God is the source of all good things in our lives. Forgetting to say thank you is not only ungrateful—it's downright rude!

Sadly, we often do just that. Getting so busy thinking about what we want next, we forget the blessings we already have—and who gave them to us.

Supplication. Now—in its proper place—comes the time to bring our requests before our Father. Because—having thought about God's perfection . . . our longing to be close to him . . . our sorrow for our sins . . . our gratitude for his loving care—*now* we are prepared. *Now* we begin to see that the purpose of supplication is not to pressure God into giving us *things,* but to ask God to *help us fulfill his purpose for our lives*!

▬▬▬ THE F-A-C-T-S OF YOUR LIFE

"This is the day the LORD has made . . ." (Psalm 118:24 NIV). And what better way to celebrate it than by putting the F-A-C-T-S to work in your life!

Faith: Get to know God through Scripture. **Adoration:** Praise his glory and holiness. **Confession:** Tell him you're sorry for your sins. **Thanksgiving:** Say "thank you" . . . for *everything*. **Supplication:** Ask him to help you be everything he wants you to be!

Like to get a feeling for how the priorities of prayer fit you? Okay, pick up your Bible (you do know exactly where it is, don't you?) and look up these verses in Scripture. Read each one carefully, then jot down how they make you feel.

→ **When I read John 15:7 it made me realize that my Faith is**

→ **The words of Adoration in Psalm 150 made me want to**

→ **The words about Confession in 1 John 1:9 reminded me that**

→ **1 Thessalonians 5:16–18 brought to mind *these* reasons for Thanksgiving in my life:**

→ **"Supplication"?! Oh, my! 1 John 5:14–15 is so much different than these things I usually ask for:**

D7

DAY8

So Why Ask?

We can come to God with no doubts. This means
that when we ask God for things (and those things
agree with what God wants for us), then God cares
about what we say. God listens to us every time we ask him....
— 1 JOHN 5:14–15 (ICB)

Have you ever noticed how even the simplest things can turn out to be *more* than they seem at first glance? Even something as ordinary as, say, a blank sheet of paper. . . .

Write on it, and you see a message. Draw on it, and you see a piece of art. Fold it up in a certain way, sail it through the air, and . . . *Ta-Dah!* . . . an airplane! What you *see* is . . . what you look for.

It's that way with some questions, too. Sometimes there's *more* to the answer than you might expect. Which brings us back to . . . just about everybody's favorite question about prayer: If God knows what we need *before* we ask, why bother asking at all?

HERE'S WHERE THINGS GET A LITTLE COMPLICATED

The *first* part of the answer, of course, comes when we remember the primary purpose of prayer: Building a relationship with God. (Which also answers the "Why pray at all?" question.)

So far, so good, right? But if prayer is not meant to be all about "asking," does that mean we shouldn't ask at *all*?

Not at all.

You see, God not only ordains the ends (the results), but also the *means*—the actions that lead to those results. And prayer is *action!* Prayer is *our* part of the process. So, in a way, asking, "Why pray, if God knows what we need?" is the same as asking, "Why get dressed and go to school every day?" or "Why wash my hands?" or "Why pull up a weed?"

Here's why: You need an education. Clean hands are a good idea. To let the flowers grow. And those things happen because *you:* Go . . . Wash . . . Weed.

BUT JUST WHEN YOU THINK YOU'VE "GOT IT" . . .

So, actions produce results. And prayer is action. End of story? Nope. Because there is a difference—a huge difference—between the results of our actions in the world and what happens as a result of our prayers!

Here in the physical world, God has set up things to happen in ways that produce predictable results. Do *this*, and *that* happens. Wash your hands, and they're clean. Pull out a weed, and it's gone. Drop something, and it falls (the old Gravity Game!).

BUT, FORTUNATELY FOR US . . .

Prayer works differently. God has kept for himself alone the power to decide what will happen with our prayer requests. Which is all that stands between us and total disaster! *Because God* always *gives us what is best for us—even when what we ask for is not!*

In the same way your parents put away sharp pointy objects when you were a baby . . . or discouraged your later attempts to "fly" from the roof . . . God protects us from ourselves!

Your prayers *are* answered . . . and always in the best possible way, by the loving Father who wants nothing but good for you.

Go ahead and ask. God doesn't mind. Because when we ask, we are reminded how much we depend on him. And that alone is a *very* good reason for praying.

D8

Next time you're feeling a little disappointed because God hasn't "answered" a prayer, you might try a little mental review of some other— *really* important!—things you've asked him for in the past. And what would have happened *if* . . .

→ **Oh, yes, I remember when I asked God for**

→ **And when it didn't happen, I felt**

→ **But now I see that**

DAY 9

Building Our Relationship with God

Lord, you have examined me. You know all about me. You know when I sit down and when I get up. You know my thoughts before I think them.

— PSALM 139:1–2 (ICB)

Relationships. Friendships. Life would feel very empty without them, wouldn't it?

So—because we're pretty smart cookies—we treat our friendships with the care and respect they deserve. We spend time on them. We put a lot of ourselves into them. We make it clear how important they are to us.

Usually. Most of the time. Except . . . except *maybe* when it comes to the most important friendship of all: Our relationship with God! A lot of people are "all thumbs" when it comes to that relationship of *all* relationships. They feel shy . . . or unworthy . . . or uncertain how to *talk* to God.

Which is a shame. Because Jesus not only told us how—*and* gave us the words—he *showed* us!

▰▰▰ A "BEGINNER'S GUIDE" TO FRIENDSHIP WITH GOD

It's all there—everything we need to know about communicating with God—in the Prayer of Jesus. It is the perfect prayer. It is also the prayer that is most often ignored . . . or recited without thought . . . and sometimes even forgotten!

Yet Jesus himself said *this* is the way to talk to God. ". . . When you pray, you should pray like this . . ." (Matthew 6:9 ICB).

D9

Did Jesus model the principles of this prayer in his *own* prayer life? Absolutely!

Jesus *lived out* every element of the prayer!

■■■■■ THE AWESOME POWER OF EXAMPLE

Jesus demonstrated—by his actions—the *reality* behind the words of his prayer. In fact, Jesus' entire life *was* the prayer!

When he taught his disciples to pray "Our Father . . . ," it was because that is what *he* called God—time after time in Scripture.

Jesus willingly bowed to God's will. In the Garden of Gethsemane, when he asked that the cup of suffering be taken from him, it was with these words: *"Yet not as I will, but as you will"* (Matthew 26:39 NIV).

And though he was the Bread of Life, he thanked God before he ate . . . before he fed the five thousand (John 6:11 NIV) . . . and when he broke bread with his disciples during the Last Supper (Matthew 26:26 NIV).

Jesus asked forgiveness for our debts through his death on the cross, and also forgave those who had wronged him.

And he spoke from personal experience when he taught the disciples to pray, "And lead us not into temptation, but deliver us from the evil one." Because he, too, had been tempted by the Devil during his forty days and forty nights in the desert.

■■■■■ MORE THAN A FORMULA

In his prayer, Jesus gave so much more than just a "formula" for prayer. He gave us a *living example* of a perfect relationship with God.

Jesus has "been there." He has "done that." And because he has, his prayer is as perfect a "fit" for our lives today as it was when he spoke the words two thousand years ago.

The most wonderful relationship of all *can* be yours. Are you ready to begin?

Example is a very powerful—and trustworthy—teacher. Not many people would disagree about that. But have you ever *really* thought about ways that examples—good *and* bad—have worked in *your* life? Take a look; you might be surprised.

→ **These are some positive things I've learned by example:**

→ **Because of this example, I decided I would never . . . *ever***

→ **I have been an example to others when I**

27

D9

DAY10

"Our Father in Heaven . . ."

Yet to all who received him,
to those who believed in his
name, he gave the right to
become children of God. . . .
— JOHN 1:12 (NIV)

Could there possibly *be* a more comfortable—and *comforting*—way to begin a prayer than by calling on the love of a father with absolute trust and confidence?

Yet for the disciples, the opening words of the Prayer of Jesus must have been nothing less than . . . *shocking*. Of all the things they had ever learned about prayer, this was certainly not one of them!

Call God "our Father"?! The name of God was so sacred to the Jewish people that they were not permitted to even speak it out loud. How could they *dare* call him "our Father" now? Yet that is exactly how Jesus taught the disciples to pray.

A PRIVILEGE . . . AND A JOY

There was, however, a catch. As John explains, only those who accepted Jesus and believed in him had the right to call God "our Father." To the people who believed in him, Jesus ". . . gave the right to become children of God" (John 1:12 ICB).

In fact, Jesus made it perfectly clear that there were only *two* kinds of people in the world: those who should refer to Satan as "our father" and those who may call God "our Father" (John 8:44–47 ICB).

The privilege, and the joy, of being children of God comes to us through Jesus—the only true-born Son of God. *Through faith in Jesus*, we become God's sons and daughters by adoption (Romans 8)!

■■■■ "F" IS FOR FAITH

"Our Father. . . ." It's not by accident that Jesus began his prayer with these words. He could have said "O Mighty God . . ." or "O Glorious Creator. . . ." But instead, he gave us words of faith in a father's love as the foundation for our relationship with God.

And when he added ". . . in heaven," he was reminding us of the infinite wonder of God, who is beyond all space and time.

"Our Father in heaven. . . ." Words of faith on which to build our relationship with God. Words of reverence and respect to make us mindful of *our* place in that relationship.

When we say these words, we are doing *more* than just "getting God's attention." We are declaring our faith in the wisdom and goodness of the One who created us and holds us close and safe.

■■■■ HELD SAFE IN LOVING HANDS

Remember how safe you felt as a baby in your parents' arms? Or how strong your dad's hands were when he whisked you off that tumbling bike? Or how a "Mom" smile and hug could make a *really bad day* not so bad after all?

Remember how that felt? No? Well, it *is* kind of easy to forget those moments now that you're all grown up (and you and the adults in your life don't *always* see eye to eye on things).

Still, when push comes to shove, it *is* kind of nice to know there's someone always there for you—no matter what—isn't it?

God is there for you in that way, too. If you invite him to be. And you *begin* by calling his name. With love. And faith. And respect. And reverence.

D10

"Our Father in heaven. . . ." Surprising, isn't it, that four little words could say so much? But that's the amazing thing about focusing your attention on the idea of faith. You discover all *kinds* of things about God . . . and about yourself. And there's no better place to do that than in the words of Scripture.

→ **I asked three people I admire their favorite Scripture about God, and they said:**

→ **My favorite passage about God is**

→ **When I think about really talking to God as a father, I**

WanNa wriTe moRe? UsE tHe PraYer TracKer tHat staRts On pAge 91
tO tRacK yOur prayEr prAisEs aNd reQueSts.

D10

DAY 11

"Hallowed Be Your Name . . ."

*"This, then, is how you should
pray: 'Our Father in
heaven, hallowed be
your name . . .'"*
— MATTHEW 6:9 (NIV)

First things first. . . ." How often have you heard *that?!* Probably every time you get "sidetracked," right?

But, you know—aggravating as it might be the umpteenth time you hear it—it *is* very good advice. Because it keeps you focused on what is important! Just as Jesus did with this next phrase in his prayer.

To pray "hallowed be your name" puts the emphasis on God *first*— exactly where it belongs. It reminds us that our daily lives should reflect a commitment to God's nature and holiness, rather than to our own needs.

"A" IS FOR ADORATION

With these words of praise, we worship and adore God's unique holiness. We pray that his name will be honored and respected by all people everywhere; that his Word will be preached clearly and truly; that our churches will be led by faithful pastors and preserved from false prophets.

With these words, we remind *ourselves* that everything is meaningless unless God's name is magnified!

But that's not *all* the words do . . . !

When we pray "hallowed be your name," we are asking that we might

31

D11

make every day of our lives a "song" of praise for God—in everything we say and *do*. And we are pledging that, rather than seek honor for ourselves, we will seek that God's name be glorified and made holy.

BUT ISN'T GOD'S NAME ALREADY HOLY?

The answer is obvious: a resounding "Yes!" But that doesn't mean it's not a good question. In fact, people have been asking for centuries why we should pray for something that is already accomplished.

Here's how Augustine, one of the early church fathers, answered: "This is prayed for not as if the name of God were not holy already, but that it may be held holy by men . . . *that God may become so known to them* that they shall reckon nothing more holy. . . ."

And there's something *else* that makes these words special. They are timeless! They will never go out of date. Even in heaven—when we are no longer concerned with things like "daily bread" or temptation—we will still continue to praise and adore God's holy name.

And there's another "something else," too. These are *also* words of celebration—celebration of our *right*, through Jesus' sacrifice, to even say these words in the first place!

CELEBRATING THE WONDERFUL

We all admire what is worthy and good. And love to say so!

That classmate who is *everything* we'd like to be. Selfless people, like the late Mother Teresa, who live to serve others. New York City fire, police, and rescue workers. An athlete who might not always win but *always* gets up again.

Think of them, and the words of admiration just bubble up, because we know "wonderful" when we see it!

How much more, then, should we celebrate—and make holy the name of—the One who is the source of *all* things wonderful!

You could probably, without much trouble, make a list of people *you* admire. People you know. People you only know of. You could probably also come up with some very good reasons why.

But has it ever occurred to you to put *God* on that list? Or to think about reasons why he should be at the very top? Even more important, has it ever occurred to you to tell him so?! Opens up some interesting thoughts, doesn't it?

→ I admire these things about my "heroes":

→ These things about God make me want to shout with joy:

→ For one day I am going to pray only prayers of praise, because God

33

DAY 12

"Your Kingdom Come . . ."

> *Jesus said, "My kingdom does not belong to this world. If it belonged to this world, my servants would fight so that I would not be given over to the Jews. But my kingdom is from another place."*
>
> —JOHN 18:36 (ICB)

The phrase "your kingdom come" shines with such gold and glory it can take your breath away. Imagine: God's kingdom, right here on earth . . . every moment filled with the unending joy and delight of his holy presence! Who *wouldn't* long for heaven on earth?!

Here's a news flash: Heaven once *did* exist on earth! But it didn't last long. When the first human beings sinned in Eden, our world was plunged into darkness.

Ever since, the history of earth has been a war between two kingdoms. An early church father called them the kingdom of God . . . and the kingdom of man.

■■■■ BATTLEFIELD EARTH!

The kingdom of man might *sound* glorious, but the truth is far different. Because of sin, humankind was chained to a dark destiny.

Then God sent his Son into the world to overthrow the Devil's domain with his message of salvation . . . and his sacrifice on the cross.

But the hearts of men were stubborn, and they were *used to* darkness! Jesus came to establish an eternal kingdom. But people only wanted an earthly king who would defeat their enemies by military might.

And when Jesus said, "My kingdom is not of this world" (John 18:36 NIV), the shouts of "Hosanna! . . . Blessed is the King of Israel!" (John 12:13 NIV) became screams of "Crucify him! . . . We have no king but Caesar!" (John 19:15 NIV). They wanted an earthly king. Jesus had come to take his place on the throne of their *hearts*.

CHOOSING SIDES!

With the words "your kingdom come," Jesus was teaching us to ask our heavenly Father to rule over the territory of our hearts!

The words are also an *invitation*—to us—to bring the kingdom of Christ into every part of our lives.

And they are something *else*, too: *A pledge of allegiance*! When we pray "your kingdom come," we are choosing sides! We are "signing up" on God's team . . . and promising to throw ourselves, heart and soul, into expanding Christ's kingdom, rather than our own earthly concerns.

VICTORY . . . AND BEYOND

The truth is: Christ has *already* won the victory. He *has* defeated the darkness.

The reality is: Not everybody knows it!

And until they do—until everyone welcomes Christ into his or her heart—the battle continues.

It's like being on a team that has already made the decisive play of the game. Victory is "in the bag."

Does that mean the other team is just going to give up and go home? Does that mean *you* can start to slack off?

Well, you are locked in the battle of all time right now. And the enemy is strong . . . and stubborn . . . *and* he fights dirty!

But God is on *your* side. Dig in, and fight the good fight!

D12

Does it surprise you to learn that you have a part to play in the battle against Evil? A part much bigger than simply conquering your own sins and shortcomings? You might want to give some serious thought to how that makes you feel.

→ **Me?! Have a part in bringing God's kingdom to earth? Wow, that's pretty**

→ **In a really *big* battle, I wonder if I would be able to**

→ **When I pray "your kingdom come," I understand I am telling God I will**

DAY 13

"Your Will Be Done . . ."

Then Jesus walked a little farther away
from them. He fell to the ground and prayed,
"My Father, if it is possible, do not give me
this cup of suffering. But do what you want,
not what I want."

— MATTHEW 26:39 (ICB)

Do what you want, not what I want."

Wow! Is there anything *harder* for us stubborn, absolutely-positive-we-know-best humans than to let someone *else* call the shots?

We want to choose. We want to decide. We want to be in charge! And we always have—right from the start.

Eve wanted to make up her *own* mind about that juicy piece of fruit. Cain had his *own* version of "brotherhood." And King David had his *own* ideas about God's will . . . never mind what the prophet Nathan had to say on the subject.

Yes, giving up control *is* one of the hardest things to do. It is also one of the most *important* things to do . . . if we are to pray Jesus' prayer with honesty and trust.

THE WORDS THAT SET US FREE

When we pray "your will be done," we are recognizing that God is in control of the world and our lives . . . and that he knows, always, what is best for us.

Something else happens, too, with these words. We are reminded that we must submit our wills to God's will. And that takes practice! But once

37

we get the knack, wonderful things happen. We have the comfort—and *freedom*—of living with absolute trust and confidence in *the One who created us*. We don't have to worry . . . about anything. God is in charge!

▮▮▮▮ WITH EVERY PROBLEM . . . A GIFT

Finally, when we pray—as Jesus did—"not my will, but thy will be done," we accept that life might not always be easy. There will be trials. There will be troubles. But seeing them as part of God's plan frees us to put them to work *for* us.

We discover our greatest sorrows can turn out to be our greatest opportunities to become stronger, *better* people.

▮▮▮▮ LEMONADE, ANYONE . . . ?

When you get right down to it, we have *two* choices when life hands us "lemons." We can pucker up and complain that things "aren't fair." Or . . . we can make lemonade! Same lemons. It's what we *do* with them that makes the difference.

But what *is* it that makes us react one way . . . or the other? I suspect that the people who taste only the "bitter" are people who are *totally surprised* that bad things could ever happen to *them*.

And the people who take life's trials—and tragedies—and find a way to turn them into something sweet and good? Ah . . . *they* are the ones who are prepared. Because they accept life's ups—*and* downs—as part of God's plan.

When you pray "your will be done" . . . you are putting yourself in God's hands with complete trust that ". . . in everything God works for the good of those who love him. They are the people God called, because that was his plan" (Romans 8:28 ICB).

You are saying, "I might not always like what happens, Lord, but I accept whatever you choose to send me."

You are *preparing* yourself . . . to become one of life's great lemonade-makers!

When the worst—or what *seems* like the worst—happens in your life, how do *you* react? Does it throw you for a loop . . . or are you able to find ways to cope? When you pray about your problems, is it only to ask God to make them "go away"? Have you *ever* asked him instead to help you understand his purpose in what happens?!

→ **When** _____ **happened, I felt as if**

→ **Here's what I tried to do about it:**

→ **If I had remembered that God is always "in charge," I might have**

"On Earth As It Is in Heaven . . ."

*But seek first his kingdom
and his righteousness,
and all these things will
be given to you as well.*

— MATTHEW 6:33 (NIV)

There's that word again: *Heaven.* We've barely begun the Prayer of Jesus and already we've tackled the idea of heaven *three times!*

We began with "Our Father in heaven." Then we called heaven to earth when we prayed "your kingdom come." And now we ask that God's will be done "on earth as it is in heaven." Why? Why this repetition of the idea of heaven?

Surely God knows his own "address"?

And hasn't he already made it perfectly clear how very much he *longs* to bring heaven to earth?

And doesn't it go without saying that doing his will is the joy and delight of heaven's citizens? Can there be any doubt that God is *very* aware of heaven?

Yes, God is. The question is: Are we? Do *we* live each day with heaven in mind?

BEFORE THE JOURNEY . . . THE DESTINATION

It's not by accident that Jesus directs our attention to heaven. He knew that getting where we want to go begins with . . . knowing *where* we want to get! So he taught us to focus *on* the idea of heaven, because that will one day be our eternal home.

D14

You might even say he was helping us develop the right perspective. And you could absolutely say he was helping us set *priorities!*

▰▰▰ GETTING OUR PRIORITIES STRAIGHT

With his repeated reminders of heaven, Jesus helps us move into the right frame of mind for talking with God. When we think first of the glory and majesty of the Lord of all creation, our own little wants and needs and "must-haves" fall neatly into their *proper* place.

And, yes, our needs and desires—even our "must-haves"—*do* have a place. God is our loving *Father,* remember? He wants us to have the things we need . . . but most of all he wants us to be holy!

And when we come before him with love and respect and reverence— mindful of whom we are talking to—he is more than ready to hear our requests.

▰▰▰ THE HEAVEN/EARTH "CONNECTION"

There's something else you should know about these words. They are the "balance point" of the prayer . . . the place where heaven touches earth in our thoughts.

Ever walked a seesaw board? Just for fun? You begin by looking—and moving—*upward*, away from the earth. As you climb, the board begins to shift. Finally, right at the center point, the board is level and you are per- fectly balanced between the ground below . . . and the heavens above. (Seeing things from a fresh point of view!)

Then, you take one more step . . . the board tilts down . . . a few quick steps . . . and your feet are back on the ground.

The Prayer of Jesus helps us find that perfect balance, too. It lifts us upward with thoughts of heaven . . . gives us a fresh point of view on our rela- tionship with God . . . then brings us back to the things of earth. Where—with heaven in mind—we are *now* ready to bring our requests to God.

D14

Who would have dreamed that a few little words—"on earth as it is in heaven"—could say so *much?!* But, you know, when we make it a point to keep heaven in mind *every* day—remember to look at things in a "heavenly" light—amazing things start to happen. Take today, for instance. . . .

→ _____ **happened today, and I felt**

→ **But when I try to see it from a heavenly point of view, I realize**

→ **Below are three things I can do to keep heaven in mind every day:**

DAY15

Bringing Our Requests

So I tell you, continue to ask, and God
will give to you. Continue to search,
and you will find. Continue to knock,
and the door will open for you.

—LUKE 11:9 (ICB)

So, here you are . . . at the moment in prayer when you can bring your requests before God. And, all of a sudden, you're tongue-tied!

Could it be that the idea of God's awesome majesty makes you feel a little . . . shy?

Or are you wondering how the One who hung the moon and stars could possibly be interested in—and have time for—the details of *your* life?

Don't worry. He *is* interested. He *does* have time. True, our wants and needs *are* pretty little in the grand scheme of the universe . . . but they are *not* little in God's eyes. And, yes, it's right that we feel humble . . . right that we think carefully about what is important . . . but it's also very *all right* to ask God for things!

▨ SOMEONE WE CAN COUNT ON

Jesus himself told us we can always count on our Father's loving care.

Remember that moment in Luke 11:1 when the disciples begged Jesus to teach them to pray? Well, *of course* he would! But *first* there was something very important they needed to understand. So Jesus pulled out a parable—one of his all-time favorite ways of "making a point."

He began with a story about a man who had unexpected company late

43

at night . . . and not a thing to eat in the house! So he knocks on his neighbor's door and asks to borrow three loaves of bread.

What?! The disciples had *no* idea where Jesus was going with this. Okay, asking a neighbor for help made sense. There were no 24-hour convenience stores in those days. If you needed something in the middle of the night . . . you asked a neighbor. But what did *that* have to do with praying?!

■■■■ "ASK AND IT WILL BE GIVEN TO YOU . . ."

Jesus just smiled and went on, telling them how the neighbor shouted back, "Go away!" It was late. His kids were asleep. He couldn't help.

"But," Jesus said, "if that man had kept knocking, his neighbor *would* have given him the bread . . . if only to make him stop bothering him."

Jesus looked at the disciples, smiling. They looked back, confused.

So Jesus spelled it out. "So I say to you: ask and it will be given to you; seek and you will find; knock and the door will be opened to you. . . ."

If your grumpy neighbor offers you help—if only to make you go away—how much more will your heavenly Father, who is righteous and loving, come to your aid when you ask.

■■■■ THE LIGHT DAWNS . . .

Oh. Of course! Now they get it. If that neighbor ended up helping—*even for a less than noble reason*—they could *certainly* count on God . . . who *loved* them!

So go ahead. Ask. God will *never* shout, "Go away!" What you *will* hear (if you listen) is, "Come on in . . . tell me what you need."

Surprised? You shouldn't be. Haven't there been times when you've asked someone who cares about you for some *huge* favor you didn't really deserve? And the answer—incredibly!—was "Yes"!

And that was out of *human* love. Imagine what *God* will do!

D15

Are you ever uncomfortable about asking for things? Some people would rather eat worms than ask anyone for anything. And then there are those who rattle off requests at the drop of a hat (which they had also asked for). Most of us fall somewhere in between.

What about you? And what about when it comes to asking *God?*

→ **I find asking for things (pick one)**

○ **Hard**   ○ **Easy**   ○ **Never thought about it**

because

→ **When I asked _____ for _____, I was totally amazed**

→ **When I think about asking God for things, I feel**

WanNa wriTe moRe? UsE tHe PraYer TracKer tHat staRts On pAge 91 tO tRacK yOur prayEr prAisEs aNd reQueSts.

D15

DAY 16

"Give Us Today Our Daily Bread . . ."

"Even though you are bad, you know how to give good things to your children. So surely your heavenly Father knows how to give the Holy Spirit to those who ask him."
— LUKE 11:13 (ICB)

Now comes the moment when Jesus gives the disciples the first words of "asking." And what *is* it that he teaches them to ask for? Bread!

Kind of a surprising first request, right? There were certainly a lot of other things they were going to need. Things like wisdom . . . or holiness . . . or courage . . . or protection from their enemies. But Jesus went right to the most basic human need of all with "give us today our daily bread."

Maybe you've never thought that bread was very important. And—in our fast-food, grocery-store-on-every-corner, have-another-snack world—maybe it's not.

But in Jesus' world, bread was the foundation of *life* itself. Indeed, Jesus has been called the Bread of Life. And even today, in many parts of the world, there are people who would give *anything* to know where *their* next crust of bread is coming from!

NOT BY BREAD ALONE . . .

Yes, it's a very simple request . . . with an astonishing "extra added benefit." Jesus knew exactly what he was doing. In teaching the disciples to trust God to provide the most basic necessity of life, he was preparing them to *also* receive a gift beyond price!

And just to be sure they were clear on the differences between relationships among neighbors . . . and the special relationship a father has with his children . . . Jesus expanded on his "grumpy neighbor" story.

"Which of you fathers," he asked them, "if your son asks for a fish, will give him a snake instead? Or if he asks for an egg, will give him a scorpion?

"If you then, though you are evil, know how to give good gifts to your children, how much more will your Father in heaven give the Holy Spirit to those who ask him!" (Luke 11:11–13 NIV).

MORE THAN ANYONE COULD POSSIBLY ASK

The gift of the Holy Spirit! Jesus had just moved his story to a whole new level.

For centuries the Jewish people had been taught that God was remote and unapproachable. *Now* Jesus was telling them God cares for us as tenderly as a father cares for his own dear children. And when we trust him to take care of our needs, he will never, ever, give us anything harmful.

Then he added the final words that must have sent a shiver up the disciples' spines: ". . . the Holy Spirit!"

With those words, he was promising that we can trust in God to feed *more* than our bodies. He will feed our souls!

BEYOND YOUR WILDEST DREAMS . . .

Scripture doesn't say *how* the disciples reacted. I suspect they just stood there, mouths open, trying to understand what they had done to deserve *this*.

Kind of like *you* would if you were expecting a new CD . . . and got an all-expense-paid trip to the Grammy Awards instead. Or asked for a ride to soccer practice . . . and were handed the keys to the family car! Stunned. Amazed. And very—*very*—excited!

D16

Trust is a very delicate thing . . . and a very *risky* business. It takes a *huge* leap of faith to trust that something—or someone—won't disappoint us. And, of course, they sometimes do (just as the very-human-*you* sometimes does, too), which makes it all that much harder to trust the next time—because you can never be completely *sure*. . . .

But one place you can put yourself with 100 percent absolute confidence is in God's hands. But have you? *Can* you? Or is trust a really big "issue" in your life?

→ **Here's the most awful "broken trust" in my life:**

→ **Because of that I**

→ **When I think of relying totally and completely on God for** *everything,* **I**

"Daily Bread" Is *More* Than Just Something to Eat

Then Jesus declared, "I am the bread of life. He who comes to me will never go hungry, and he who believes in me will never be thirsty."

—JOHN 6:35 (NIV)

Have you ever opened . . . and opened . . . and opened . . . a set of "nesting" dolls? Inside each one is . . . something *else* to discover. It's that way with Jesus' stories, too. Like his parable about the three loaves . . .

First, he lets the disciples know that asking—making their needs known—is okay.

Next, he surprises them with the news that God is *not* distant and uncaring—but their loving *Father*. Then, he *dazzles* them with the promise—"for those who ask"—of the gift of the Holy Spirit!

And *that* opens up a whole new layer of thinking. Because when God gives the Holy Spirit, he is giving . . . *everything!*

■■■■ LITTLE WORD . . . BIG MEANING

In that same way, the "daily bread" in Jesus' prayer represents a lot *more* than just food. Christian thinkers through the centuries agree: The word *bread* stands for *everything* necessary to life. But rather than having us list every shoe . . . roof . . . crop in the field . . . Jesus packed all those necessities into one word: Bread.

And kindly note another word, too: Necessities. We are talking the *basics* of life here, not the frills and "extras," that we might—or might not—get. But what we *can* count on, when we trust in God, are the things we really *need* . . . including "food" for our spirits.

■■ LOOKING OUTSIDE OURSELVES

Here's something else worth our attention. It's "give **us** this day **our** daily bread." Jesus did *not* say "me" and "my." With "us" and "our," he tells us to look outside ourselves . . . and see the needs of others, too!

Sometimes we need reminding. Oh, it's not that we don't *know* there are people who are hungry . . . lonely . . . afraid. We have only to turn on the television news to see their faces, and—for a moment—share their pain.

Then a commercial comes on, or we change channels . . . and get on with our comfortable lives. Maybe with a quick prayer of thanks that *we* don't have to suffer like that.

Sorry . . . that's *not* enough! Counting our blessings is not *enough*. We have to make our blessings *count!*

■■■ FROM WHOM MUCH IS GIVEN, MUCH IS EXPECTED

Jesus made that very clear in another story about a rich man who received everything . . . and *gave* nothing. And he cut *that* attitude absolutely *no* slack! "You fool! This very night your life will be demanded from you" (Luke 12:20 NIV). And he might as well have added: "And what have you done with it?"

Jesus always chose his words with care. And in "give us this day our daily bread" he reminds us that we must care about more than ourselves.

Which means, when you think about it, throwing yourself into collecting food for the hungry . . . or volunteering for a senior center . . . or taking time to smile and say "Hi" to that shy kid *nobody* talks to . . . aren't just "nice" things to do. They are *necessary* things!

After all, how can we ask God to *give* to us, unless we are *givers*, too?

D17

When you look in the mirror, what do you see? *You*, right? Maybe, on a good day, with a smile (carefully constructed to hide those braces!). On a not-so-good day, it might be you with a frown, or an expression of worry, or frustration. But always . . . you.

But what if you tried seeing "you" in a bigger way . . . as part of a *family* that includes *all* God's children?! It *could* make you think in a new way about what's important . . . what's necessary . . . and what your "brothers and sisters" might need that *you* can give.

→ When I think of others when I pray, it's usually

→ It never occurred to me that Jesus expects me to

→ I would probably be more aware of others' needs, if I would make a point to

DAY 18

"Forgive Us Our Debts . . ."

God, be merciful to me because you are
loving. Because you are always ready to
be merciful, wipe out all my wrongs. Wash
away all my guilt and make me clean again.
I know about my wrongs. I can't forget
my sin.

—PSALM 51:1–3 (ICB)

Have you ever noticed how brilliant we are at coming up with "reasons" and excuses for the not-so-nice things we do—convincing ourselves they're not *really* so bad after all?

Reality check! Much as we'd like to think we're "pretty good," the truth is that *we all sin*. Sometimes it's things we do. Other times it's things we *fail* to do.

Hey, we're only human! you might be thinking right about now. And that's absolutely true. That's also absolutely the *problem*. Because ever since the Garden of Eden, we humans have a dreadful tendency to give in to our darker sides.

We sin. We hurt others. We hurt ourselves. Worst of all, we hurt God—who sacrificed his Son to *free* us from sin.

MAKING THINGS "RIGHT"

So, how *do* we wash away the stains left by the nasty little—and big—things we do? How do we make amends to God? We do what Jesus taught us to do!

We come before our Father and humbly ask, "Forgive us our debts." We ask him to wipe away all we owe him for the pain our sins cause him. But before we can do that, something *else* has to happen. We have to know *what* it is we are asking forgiveness for! And that means doing something very hard. . . .

We have to stop kidding *ourselves!* The first step on the road to forgiveness is taking an honest look at our faults . . . admitting them to ourselves. It's not always easy, but we *can* do it.

You can do it. You can take time at the end of every day to really *think* about those things you'd rather just forget. It's not always a pretty picture. But it is one you need to see clearly in order to take the next step on the road to forgiveness.

■■■■ "C" IS FOR CONFESSION

Confession—admitting our faults to God—is one of the key, and very necessary, elements of prayer.

It's not that God doesn't already know exactly what you've done. He does.

That impatient, don't-bother-me look when a new kid at school said a hopeful "Hi." God saw it. That "creative" story (Lie!) about what *really* happened at the mall. God heard it. Those glances at your neighbor's paper during that test you didn't study for. God knows cheating when he sees it!

It's not God who needs a list of your sins. It's *you*. Because unless you come before him with your sins clearly in mind, "forgive us our debts" is just a string of empty words. And Jesus didn't use *any* empty words in his prayer. Everything he taught us to say is there for a reason. Everything. Including the *rest* of the "forgiveness" phrase.

■■■■ AND ONE MORE THING . . .

Yes, there is more. Seven more words that come right after "forgive us our debts." Seven words that make forgiveness . . . *possible*. Seven words so important they deserve a chapter all to themselves!

D18

Maybe you've never thought of sin as being some kind of "debt" . . . something you *owe* God for. And maybe you've even wondered why Jesus used that word, instead of just having us say "forgive us our *sins*." Or maybe you find the whole idea a little confusing. Maybe it might be a good idea to think some more about all that!

→ **Being "in debt" means that I**

→ **Since sin *is* a debt, I realize now that I owe God—big time—for**

→ **Here's why I'm so very thankful that through his sacrificial death on my behalf Jesus has paid completely the debt I owe God:**

DAY 19

"... As We Also Have Forgiven Our Debtors"

"And when you stand praying, if
you hold anything against anyone,
forgive him, so that your Father in
heaven may forgive you your sins."

— MARK 11:25 (NIV)

As we also have forgiven our debtors. . . ." There they are—the *rest* of the words Jesus gave us to use in asking God's forgiveness. The words that make the prayer *work!*

Until we put these words right after "forgive us our debts," our prayer is not complete. Because forgiveness is a *two-way* street! Or to put it another way: "What goes around, comes around!"

When he gave us these words, Jesus was making it clear that before we can expect God to forgive us, *we* have to be ready to forgive others. Because what these words are *really* saying to God is: Treat me in exactly the same way *I* treat other people!

Sound kind of familiar? It should.

■■■ A RULE AS GOOD AS GOLD

Remember the Golden Rule? "So in everything, do to others what you would have them do to you . . ." (Matthew 7:12 NIV). It's one of the most beautiful—and powerful—pieces of advice Jesus gave. (And one that could keep the world out of *a lot* of trouble if everyone paid attention to it!)

In the forgiveness request, however, the idea advances a step *further*. And it now could read, "do to others what you would have *God* do to you."

A FATEFUL DECISION

To make sure we'd take seriously our responsibility to forgive others, Jesus told a story about two debtors. The first owed his master something like twenty million dollars. The second debtor owed the first less than twenty dollars.

When the day of reckoning came, the master wiped away every penny of the multimillion-dollar debt. But was that debtor overwhelmed with gratitude? Not so you'd notice.

Instead, he tracked down the one who owed him the tiny debt and demanded, "Pay up!" And when the man couldn't, he dragged him off to debtors' prison!

When the master heard this, his judgment was swift and just. The ungrateful servant was thrown into jail until he could pay *his* debt in full—which would be . . . never!

"This," Jesus said, "is how my heavenly Father will treat each of you unless you forgive your brother from your heart" (Matthew 18:35 NIV).

The disciples got the point. The debts we owe one another are like twenty-dollar bills compared to the infinite debt we owe our heavenly Father.

God himself hung on the cross to pay for our sins. But did he blame us . . . hold a grudge? You know he didn't. Instead he loved us . . . and forgave us. How can we—how *dare* we—do less?

LOOKING FOR OPPORTUNITIES . . . AND USING THEM

Asking God for forgiveness with an *unforgiving* heart just doesn't work! And there really *are* no excuses. It's not as if we don't have plenty of opportunities every day to exercise our forgiveness "muscle."

That friend who dropped you for someone "cooler". . . . The way your brother laughed at your not-very-successful new haircut. . . . That unfair grade. . . .

You get the idea. You also get the opportunity—every time something hurtful happens—to practice what *you* ask God to do for you!

Like any skill we practice, forgiveness takes plenty of . . . practice. It's not something that comes all that naturally. Let's face it, a lot of times we'd much rather hug our hurts . . . think about them a lot . . . and, in general, make things pretty tough on the people who caused them. But we *can* change. We can look at these hurtful things that happen and—instead of seeing them as "downers"—we can recognize them as opportunities to take the high road. And forgive. It's all a matter of attitude.

→ **When someone hurts me, the first thing I want to do is**

→ **But if I tried to see injuries as "opportunities" instead, I might**

→ **Here's a time I did forgive someone, and it felt**

57

D19

DAY20

The Compassion Award

*For if you forgive men when
they sin against you, your
heavenly Father will also
forgive you.*

— MATTHEW 6:14 (NIV)

Sometimes God teaches his lessons in the most *unexpected* ways. . . .

I was in my office, playing frantic "catch-up" on an overdue book deadline when—**RING!!!**

"Where are you?" exclaimed a familiar voice on the phone.

Uh-oh. I knew that tone. It was my wife, Kathy, and—like any well-trained husband—I knew instantly that I was in serious trouble.

Was I ever! She was at my daughter's school, where Christina was receiving a Compassion Award, an event I had faithfully promised Christina—that very morning—I would attend.

I jumped into my car, sped to school, and arrived . . . too late. The ceremony was over. My heart sank. Not only had I missed an important moment in my daughter's life, but *now* I was even further behind on my book deadline, too!

But I was in for a surprise . . . or three.

MORE THAN I DESERVED . . .

I was not looking forward to seeing the you-should-have-been-here look on my wife's face. Even more, I dreaded the look of disappointment in Christina's eyes. They both surprised me.

Kathy walked up with a big smile. "Lucky for you," she said playfully, "I caught the whole thing on tape."

"Sorry," I said sheepishly.

"That's all right, sweetheart," my wife answered. "I know how busy you are right now."

And Christina? Well *she* ran up, bounced into my arms, and kissed me on the forehead. "Sorry I missed your award," I said gently.

"That's all right, Daddy," she said, hugging me. And I could see in her eyes that she had *already* forgiven me!

■■■■■ LIVING OUT THE WORD

The minute we got home, I shoved that tape into the VCR. And when I heard what Christina's teacher had to say about my daughter, tears filled my eyes.

She talked first about what a constant source of encouragement Christina was to everyone at school—teachers *and* kids. Then she went on.

"But there's also a way that we can show compassion that *nobody* knows about but God. . . . Christina *does* what Jesus tells us all to do in Mark 11:25, when he says, 'And when you stand praying, if you hold anything against anyone, forgive him, so that your Father in heaven may forgive you your sins.'

"And that's what she does—she forgives anyone who does wrong to her. She forgives them in her heart. She talks to the Lord about it, and when she prays she knows her prayers are answered. . . ."

■■■■■ GOD MOVES IN MYSTERIOUS WAYS

As I watched, beaming with pride, it suddenly struck me—God had answered *my* prayers, too!

That morning, as I began work on a chapter on forgiveness, I had asked him to guide my thoughts. And while *I* was worrying that the unexpected time-out for Christina's award ceremony would put me even further behind on my deadline, *God* was using it—and Kathy and Christina—to give me a real-life example of forgiveness in action!

God does that, you know. A lot. Of course, *we* have to pay attention. . . .

D20

God works in our lives in many ways. It's not always a "bolt from the blue," you know. Sometimes it's through the things other people do—like the way my wife and daughter forgave me for disappointing them.

The tricky part is catching on to these "quiet lessons." We have to *really* be paying attention, if we're going to get *all* of God's messages. What about you? Are you keeping an eye out for God's hand at work in *your* life?

→ **I missed it at the time, but God might have been trying to tell me something when**

→ **God might have used *me* in someone else's life when**

→ **These are some ways I could "watch" for God at work in my life:**

D20

DAY 21

"And Lead Us Not into Temptation . . ."

The only temptations that you have are the temptations that all people have. But you can trust God. He will not let you be tempted more than you can stand. But when you are tempted, God will also give you a way to escape that temptation. Then you will be able to stand it.

—1 CORINTHIANS 10:13 (ICB)

Once again, we turn to God for help. We have already asked him to *provide* for us—with the necessities of life. And we have asked his *pardon*—for the "sin debts" we owe him. Now we ask for his *protection* when we face up to temptation.

Temptation. The word itself is so . . . *tempting.* In fact, it tempts us to use it so lightly at times that we might forget just how dangerous it is!

That extra piece of chocolate cake is "tempting." A new book by your favorite author—or the latest really cool video game—is "tempting." So is stretching the truth "just a little" to avoid a dressing-down by your dad. Or getting even with someone who hurts you. Or actually *cheating* on that math test you didn't study for. . . .

TO LIVE IS TO BE TEMPTED

Temptation, big and small, is a fact of life. And we have to deal with the results—big and small. Some temptations—though it might be better to call *those* "indulgences"—don't really hurt anyone. (Unless you consider that chocolate cake–related cavity the dentist found last week. Or a lack of homework time, because of too much playtime.)

But other temptations have very serious consequences. They can separate us from God!

So why *does* God allow us to be tempted at all?

Good question. Philosophers and theologians have discussed it for centuries. But the answer takes just *two* words: *Free will!*

THE GIFT OF CHOICE

God honors us by allowing us to choose. That doesn't mean he ignores us, or forgets about us, or doesn't care what happens to us. Far from it. He is always very clear on what is right . . . and what is not. He is always ready to lend us his strength in making a good choice. And he cares very much what happens to us.

But the *choice* is ours! Just as the choice was Adam's and Eve's in the garden. Peter's choice when he denied knowing Jesus. And Jesus' choice when *he* was tempted.

We choose. We decide, when faced with temptation, whether to give in . . . or fight! But God does not leave us to fight alone. Because we can *also* choose to ask for his protection.

When you pray "Lead us not into temptation," you are putting on the Armor of God (which we'll be talking about shortly). You are calling on the awesome power of the One who "will not let you be tempted more than you can stand," and, when you *are* tempted, will "give you a way to escape that temptation" (1 Corinthians 10:13 ICB).

ALL YOU HAVE TO DO IS ASK

Temptation is powerful. God is *more* powerful. And, with his help, so are you. You can recognize temptation when it sneaks up on you with slippery charm and smiling lies. You can see past its pretty promises to its ugly truth. You can look it right in the eye and say, "No, thanks!" You can choose.

How would you rate *your* relationship with temptation? Casual acquaintances? On-again, off-again? Constant companions?

Like the rest of us, your answer is probably, "All of the above!" It all depends on what's going on in your life—worldly *and* spiritual—at any given time. And how *prepared* you are to make choices that leave you feeling proud of yourself, instead of ashamed.

Which brings us to an even *better* question: Do you know temptation when you see it?

→ **Temptation was tapping me on the shoulder when**

→ **Next thing I knew, I**

→ **I think I handled things that way because**

D21

DAY 22

"But Deliver Us from the Evil One"

And Satan, who tricked them, was thrown
into the lake of burning sulfur with the
beast and the false prophet. There they
will be punished day and night forever and ever.
—REVELATION 20:10 (ICB)

He's slick. He's tricky. He's the father of lies. And he's got his sights set on *you!*

Yes, temptation exists. And it's brought to you—complete with bells and whistles—by Satan himself. And he's expert at what he does!

That's why the words "deliver us from the evil one" *complete* our request for God's protection. Believe me, we *need* it!

When we battle against Evil, we face the intelligence, strength, and *will* of a fallen *angel!* Our adversary is a being who once walked with God . . . until the sin of pride caused his fall from heaven. Never underestimate his determination and power!

SETTING THE RECORD STRAIGHT

On the other hand, don't *over*estimate the Devil's power, either—which often happens.

And how he must *love* it, to be thought of as the author of darkness—in the same way that God is the Author of Light! How it must puff up his pride to be seen as God's equal and *opposite*.

Wrong! God is the sovereign Author of *all* creation; Satan is an angel

God created. Satan is not the *opposite* of the Creator; he is the *counterpart* to the archangel Michael. Still, he is a powerful enemy . . . and an absolute *master* of the wicked arts of temptation. Because God *allows* him to be!

CALLING ON THE ALL-POWERFUL

When we pray "lead us not into temptation, but deliver us from the evil one," we are acknowledging that God rules over *all* things—including the temptations of Satan.

Yes, "your enemy the devil prowls around like a roaring lion looking for someone to devour" (1 Peter 5:8 NIV). But . . . he's a lion on a *leash!* And God determines the length of that leash. And its *purpose*.

Remember . . . Jesus was "led *by the Spirit* into the desert to be tempted by the devil" (Matthew 4:1 NIV). Satan was doing the tempting, but God was doing the testing! Satan used the occasion to tempt Jesus to sin; God's purpose was to demonstrate that Jesus would make the right choice.

A MATTER OF CHOICE

God allows Satan to test us, too, just as he allows us to choose how we will meet that test. Will we follow Satan in his fall? Or call on God for the strength that will carry us home to heaven?

We choose. And every time we pray "lead us not into temptation, but deliver us from the evil one," we are reminded of that choice. Reminded to look forward to the day when we will be set free from all temptations. Reminded that the time is coming when Satan will be locked forever in the place *he* chose.

Reminded that there is a place waiting for *us* in the Golden City . . . and that "Nothing impure will ever enter it, nor will anyone who does what is shameful or deceitful, but only those whose names are written in the Lamb's book of life" (Revelation 21:27 NIV).

The choice is ours.

D22

→ → → ThinGs ThaT Go "buMP" in thE NiGht

Remember when you were little and absolutely *convinced* that there was a monster lurking in your closet . . . or under your bed? And how good it felt in a parent's arms, hearing, "Don't worry, I'll take care of it."?

Then you got older and understood—with great relief—that there are "no such things." And now—NOW!—you have to face up to the fact that the monster-of-all-monsters really *is* out to get you! But don't worry, God will "take care of it" . . . if you ask him.

→ **Yikes! The Devil's after me! Got to admit, that makes me feel**

→ **The Devil's "voice" is really loud when I have to make a choice about**

→ **When faced with temptation, the very *first* thing I'm going to do is**

D22

DAY 23

Putting On Our Armor

*Put on the full armor of
God so that you can
take your stand against
the devil's schemes.*

—EPHESIANS 6:11 (NIV)

MEMO
FROM: Lord Lucifer
TO: All Minions-of-Evil
SUBJECT: Performance Review

Get with it, guys! Our objective of world domination—while making major advances—has not yet been met!!!

Yes, we have pulled off some good ones—my own performance in Eden was especially brilliant—but much remains to be done. Never forget: Mankind has a great Champion . . . and a powerful Secret Weapon.

I remind you again: Beware the Armor of God!

■■■■ PREPARING FOR BATTLE

Okay, maybe it's *not* polite to read other people's mail (even if it is made up). On the other hand, it *is* an excellent idea to remind ourselves— often!—that *we* are the targets of a great plot. And the stakes are nothing less than our immortal souls!

We live in the middle of the greatest war of all times . . . Good vs. Evil. God, the all-powerful Creator, on one side. Satan on the other. And *us* in the middle . . . with an *obligation* to choose sides, and join in the battle!

Kind of a scary thought, right? And it *should* scare us. But it should also fill us with hope and courage and purpose. Because God has not left us unprotected. He sent his Son to weight the balance in our favor. And he gives us powerful *weapons* to use every day of our lives to defeat the powers of darkness.

THE ARMOR OF GOD

As knights of old faced the enemy—protected *and* prepared—God arms us for our battle against Evil. Yes, there really *is* an Armor of God. It's described right down to the last detail in Scripture.

"So stand strong, with the belt of **truth** tied around your waist. And on your chest wear the protection of **right living**. And on your feet wear the **Good News of peace** to help you stand strong. And also use the shield of **faith**. With that you can stop all the burning arrows of the Evil One. Accept God's **salvation** to be your helmet. And take the sword of the **Spirit**—that sword is the teaching of God. Pray in the Spirit at all times. Pray with all kinds of prayers, and ask for everything you need. To do this you must always be ready. Never give up. Always pray for all God's people" (Ephesians 6:14–18 ICB).

FIGHTING THE GOOD FIGHT

When we put on God's Armor we are ready to face Evil . . . and win. We have God's word on it.

". . . Then on the day of evil you will be able to stand strong. And when you have finished the whole fight, you will still be standing" (Ephesians 6:13 ICB).

That's an amazing promise! In fact, it's the only "sure thing" in life. In things of earth—no matter how much you "deserve" to win, or how noble your motives, or how big a "difference" you're trying to make—you can never know for sure how things will turn out!

But when you put on God's Armor to stand toe-to-toe with Evil . . . when the battle is finished, "you will still be standing." Guaranteed!

Were you surprised to hear about the Armor of God? Many people are. (Which is *another* good reason to spend more time in Scripture!) Yes, we know we can always call on God's help. But Evil is big, and sometimes we feel very *small* and weak.

God knows that. He also knows a prepared warrior is a *confident* warrior. And so we get a list—a very specific list—of the power at our command. Why not picture yourself—every morning—actually putting on God's Armor before you jump into the day? You'll be amazed how secure it makes you feel.

→ **I feel most protected when I think of this "piece" of God's Armor:**

→ **I feel most powerful when I put on, or pick up**

→ **And when I'm wearing *all* of God's Armor, I know for sure I can**

D23

DAY 24

Into the Deep

As the deer pants
for streams of water,
so my soul pants for
you, O God.

— PSALM 42:1 (NIV)

So . . . we've now explored every line of the Prayer of Jesus . . . dug into each phrase to uncover the rich meaning inside the simple words.

We've followed the beautiful logic, which moves us from thoughts of heaven to the things of earth.

We've traced the graceful *pattern* that flows from respect and reverence for our Creator to submission to his will . . . to sorrow for our sins . . . to entrusting ourselves to him for our earthly *and* spiritual needs.

And, as we've done so, we've begun to see *how* to talk to God in a way that creates a loving—and lasting—*relationship*.

So I guess that makes you an expert on prayer now, right?

Well . . . maybe an expert *beginner*.

■■■■ EXPLORING THE WONDERS

Your journey isn't over. It's just beginning!

Have you ever seen the ocean? (Well, of course you have! You watch TV, go to movies.) Better yet, have you ever stood *beside* the ocean? Sent your eyes—and imagination—flying over its endless blue mystery?

All it takes is one look to know . . . absolutely *know* . . . that beneath the awesome beauty of the ocean's surface lies a world of incredible wonder to explore.

D24

It's that way with God. And prayer. The deeper you let prayer carry you *into* God, the more wonders unfold for you.

STEPPING INTO THE MYSTERY

If you *have* been to the ocean, you've at least played around in the shallows near shore. And you've probably poked a curious nose into the small wonders found in tide pools. Maybe you've even put on a mask and snorkel to float, facedown, on the surface and see what lies beneath.

And there *are* marvelous things to see—even with one foot, practically, still on shore.

But what if you put on scuba gear? Ah . . . that's when *everything* changes! You trade the restless glitter and splash of the surface for the awesome silence and beauty of the deep.

And everywhere you look—a new amazement! Delicate forests of coral. Rainbows of reef fish in colors only God could imagine. The rippling grace of a stingray "flying" underwater. Gleaming "clouds" of fish that dip and glide and spin with the precision of one mind. And always—at the corner of your eye—some *new* mystery to explore.

INTO THE "DEEPS" WITH PRAYER

Many people snorkel in the shallows of prayer—and succeed only in sunburning their backs! They never quite "get it" that beneath the surface noise and distraction lies another world of silence and . . . peace.

It is in the "deeps" of prayer that our noisy "asking" gives way to the quiet beauty of a *relationship* with our Maker.

Jesus wanted that for us. He wanted us to move out of the shallows of our hearts into the boundless ocean of God's presence. So he gave us the pattern of his own personal prayer life as a shining path into the ocean of prayer.

Scuba gear for the soul, you might call it—to take us deep into the heart of the mystery . . . to truly *experience* God.

D24

Relationships that do *more* than skim the surface need time—and attention—to grow. To make them work, you have to throw yourself into them with everything you have. It's that way with your relationship with God, too.

The time comes when dipping your toe into the shallows of prayer just isn't enough. The time comes when you have to take a deep breath, trust yourself to God, and . . . *jump in!* And when you do . . . wonderful things happen!

→ **When someone uses the word *deep* about a person or idea or relationship, it makes me think**

→ **This is the best example I know of a really close, deep friendship:**

→ **If I could have a deep relationship with God, here's what I think my life would be like:**

WanNa wriTe moRe? UsE tHe PraYer TracKer tHat staRts On pAge 91 tO tRacK yOur prayEr prAisEs aNd reQueSts.

D24

DAY 25

Praying "Backward"

> *How precious to me are your thoughts,*
> *O God! How vast is the sum of them!*
> *Were I to count them, they would outnumber*
> *the grains of sand. When I awake, I am*
> *still with you.*
>
> — PSALM 139:17–18 (NIV)

Picture this: Everyone is eagerly awaiting *your* arrival as guest of honor at a fabulous party. (You, by the way, *love* being the center of attention.) So you make your "grand entrance" by . . . slipping quietly through the *back* door. *What?!*

Or maybe you're a fantastic singer giving the concert of a lifetime— which you perform . . . standing on your head. *Huh?!*

Or say you're the star of your school's track team, about to run the decisive race of the season. And you make a perfect flying start . . . from the *finish* line. *As if . . . !*

Pretty silly, right—messing up an important moment in life by turning everything upside down? *Almost* as silly as . . . praying *backward!* Who does *that?!* A lot of people.

A SLIGHT CASE OF CONFUSION

The truth is: Most of us *learned* to pray backward—looking to get *things* from God, rather than simply enjoying his presence.

We hurry into God's presence with a laundry list of prayer requests. And before our knees have barely touched the ground, we are already thinking about getting back to "real life."

73

Sadly, we often take our heavenly Father for granted. We expect a wonderful relationship without putting any time into it!

And here's the bottom line on *that:* Relationships—human *or* divine—never grow at all without spending quality time together! And that's why Jesus took such care to give us a prayer pattern that begins with building a relationship. Because that's the key to going deep with God.

██████ A CHANGE FOR THE BETTER

But before we *can* go deep with God, something else has to happen. We have to change our way of thinking about the relationship . . . shift to a fresh point of view!

And if you've ever looked through a microscope, or telescope, you know how amazing that kind of shift can be.

That ordinary—*empty*—drop of water? Put it under a microscope, magnify it a few thousand times and . . . *Ta-Dah!* . . . a whole *world* of life!

Those distant points of light in the night sky? Look at them through a telescope—better yet, take a peek through the Hubble deep-space telescope—and you've got a ringside seat at . . . Glory. The whole celestial extravaganza of creation, flung by God's hand across the universe, unfolds before your eyes.

██████ WHAT YOU SEE IS WHAT YOU GET!

Suddenly, what seemed ordinary and predictable is . . . spectacular! What happened? It's the same drop of water, the same sky. But it's not the same *you*. Your perception of things has changed—because you looked at them in a new way.

Changing the way you look at your relationship with God can be equally amazing. It can open up a glorious universe of possibility. And it can transform prayer from something you feel you "ought" to do . . . to something you can't *wait* to do!

Let's face it: We're all creatures of habit. We fall into one way of doing things or looking at things . . . and getting us to change is like pulling teeth! It's just *easier* to stick with the same old/same old. But once we *are* dragged—sometimes kicking and screaming—into a new reality, amazing things happen.

Spending time in prayer is what opens the door to a new "reality" in your relationship with God. Ready to make the shift from how you *usually* pray to how you *could* be talking to your heavenly Father?

→ **The first thing I usually think about when I pray is**

→ **The opposite of that would be to**

→ **The idea of shifting everything around makes me feel**

D25

DAY 26

"The Sounds of Silence"

"Be still, and know
that I am God. . . ."
—PSALM 46:10 (NIV)

Less talk, more action!" Ever heard that when someone wanted you to stop dawdling and "get on with it!"?

When it comes to worldly accomplishment, it's a pretty good motto. When it comes to your prayer life, here's an even better one: "Less talk, more *listening!*"

Yes, we love the sound of our own voices. But there are times when words can get seriously in the way!

Is that what happens when *you* pray? Do you turn what's supposed to be a conversation into a monologue—starring *you?*

Are your prayers filled with constant babbling? Are you deafened by your own mind-chatter? Could it be that your noisy "askings" drown out the very One you long to hear?! Has it ever occurred to you how glorious the sounds of *silence* might be?

▮▮▮▮ THE PEACE OF "QUIET"

Have you ever—after a really frantic day—just gone to your room, shut the door, and been absolutely *quiet?* In that peaceful silence, you start hearing things you usually don't notice. The song of a bird outside your window. The whisper of wind. The murmurings of your house, breathing.

Or maybe you've pressed a seashell tight against your ear . . . and heard the roar of the ocean. Of course, it's not *really* the ocean . . . it's the barrage of everyday noise amplified. It's always there, but only *heard* when you focus it with the seashell.

It's that way with God's voice, too. He's talking to you all the time, speaking to you through his Word. But *you* have to . . . listen.

LOVE LETTERS

Have you ever received a loving note from someone who cares about you? It might have been a message of support from a teacher. Or a pat on the back from a parent. Maybe even a quirky "I'm glad we're friends" rib-tickler from your best buddy. They might not be "romantic," but they *are*—for sure—love letters. Keepers. The kind you tuck away to remind you, on some "rainy day," that somebody cares.

God has written you love letters, too! Sixty-six of them, etched in heavenly handwriting . . . in the sixty-six books of the Bible. In Scripture he expresses his loving concern for you . . . and reveals everything he wants you to know about *him*.

The more time you spend with the Bible, the clearer God's voice will become . . . the more you will *hear* in prayer.

THE "VOICE" OF LOVE

It's not that you have to give up your*self* when you pray. But you do have to give up *self*ishness. Genuine prayer is not about what you can get; it's about a *union* with the Lover of your soul.

All too often we want God to give us "things." God wants to give us far more. He wants us to be still . . . so he can enlarge the territories of our *hearts*.

God speaks to you in many ways every day. In Scripture. In his actions in your life. *In the silence of your heart.* Are you listening?

D26

"Then a great and powerful wind tore the mountains apart and shattered the rocks before the LORD, but the LORD was not in the wind. After the wind there was an earthquake, but the LORD was not in the earthquake. After the earthquake came a fire, but the LORD was not in the fire. And after the fire came a gentle whisper" (1 Kings 19:11–12 NIV).

→ **I'm so used to noise in my life that the idea of silence makes me feel**

→ **This is a time when I think I really *did* hear God in prayer:**

→ **Now that I think about it, these are some things that God did in my life:**

DAY 27

The Secret Place

. . . He said to them,
"Come with me by
yourselves to a
quiet place . . ."

— MARK 6:31 (NIV)

We hear God best in the sounds of silence. Ah . . . but *where* do we find that silence in a world *filled* with noise?

Radio . . . TV . . . cell phones . . . "mail call" on the Internet . . . the cheerful—or annoying—chatter of family, friends, and total strangers . . . all compete for our attention most *all* of the time.

In fact, we're so used to this constant audio input that we sometimes feel a little uncomfortable without it. It's almost as if we find being alone with just our thoughts a little . . . scary. Yet, it's in this aloneness—this silence—that we can best hear what God has to say to us.

So, how *do* you step aside from the noise of the world—since you don't have your own private desert island? You go to your "secret place."

Secret place?! I don't have a secret place!

No problem. We can fix that. But first let's take a closer look at the *idea*.

MAYBE NOT WHAT YOU THINK . . .

The first thing to know about secret places is, there *is* no one-size-fits-all model.

There are as many kinds of secret places as there are people. My secret place is walking. My wife Kathy's is the sauna (of all places!). Joni Eareckson Tada's is her wheelchair.

79

D27

What they all share is that they are the places where we can step "outside" the sounds of this world to hear the sounds of another place . . . another voice.

That's just as Jesus did—often—when he "withdrew to lonely places and prayed" (Luke 5:16 NIV). Jesus longed for that time alone with his Father in secret.

Does that mean his work in the world wasn't important to him? Not at all. It simply means Jesus knew what was *most* important.

JUST YOU AND . . . YOU

You might not have a secret place now, but I'm pretty sure you did . . . when you were little. A place you went to be quiet . . . when the noise of the world got a little too *loud*.

Maybe it was a tree house. Or a cozy upstairs window seat. Or you, a book, and a flashlight under the sheets. It might even have been you and your "blankie"—thumb in mouth (you were *very* little, okay?)—tucked away behind the sofa.

Even today, when you're daydreaming in class, you're slipping away for a few minutes.

See? You already *are* something of an expert at tuning out the world. Now you just need to choose that special place where you can tune *in* to God.

JUST YOU AND . . . GOD

Here's the other secret about finding your secret place: You have to *want* to find it! And once you do want it, it will present itself. In fact, you'll wonder how you could have missed it for so long.

And after you've spent time *together* in there with God—pouring out your heart, and listening for his reply—you'll wonder how you ever got along without it!

You don't have to travel around the world (enticing though that idea might be) to find your own special secret place. And it doesn't have to be especially *inspirational* (remember Kathy's sauna!) or "holy" to qualify. It's God's presence that can make *any* place holy . . . and the time you spend together with him that provides the inspiration.

You might already have some ideas on where *your* "with God" place could be. Or maybe you could use a few thought-starters?

→ These are the qualities I'm looking for in my secret place:

→ Here are some of the ways I can "search" every day:

→ These are some people—who seem to have wonderful prayer lives—whom I can ask about *their* secret place:

D27

DAY 28

The Chance of a Lifetime!

*"Everyone who hears these
things I say and obeys them
is like a wise man. The wise
man built his house on rock."*
— MATTHEW 7:24 (ICB)

Lose 10 Pounds in 10 Days!" "Play Guitar Like a Pro in Just 4 Weeks!"
"Improve Your Grades Without Studying!"

Oh, how we love these sure-thing, chance-of-a-lifetime secrets of success! And, oh, how we fall—over and over again—for these empty promises that rarely come true!

My soft spot is golf. I *love* that game and have spent years trying to master it. And along the way, I've fallen for my share of faddish formulas and shortcuts to success. And you know what? I *did* get something—in fact, the *same* thing—out of every one of those win-without-work techniques: Disappointment!

"BUT IT SOUNDED SO GOOD . . ."

Unless you've been living in a cave, you know exactly what I'm talking about. Oh, you can probably walk right by the latest newfangled golf "secret" without batting an eye. But hasn't there been *something*—or a lot of somethings—that pushed *your* buttons?

Maybe it was the secret of championship soccer or how to be more popular. And who wouldn't like to draw . . . or tap-dance . . . or *whatever* . . . like a pro? Especially when you can skip over all the tough *fundamentals,* and go right to the reward!

So you buy the book or video, or send away for the gadget. And guess what? Sooner or later, the big "Gotcha!" called *reality* pops up. You're disappointed, disillusioned . . . and you *still* can't tap-dance!

THERE ARE PROMISES . . . AND PROMISES

Why am I bringing up these "what *was* I thinking?!" moments? Believe me, it's not to feel superior. (Me, with my Patented Peerless Putt-Master golf club!)

I mention all this to make a point: The world is filled with passing fancies and never-gonna-happen promises. But there is *one* promise you can absolutely count on: The Prayer of Jesus is *not* a passing fancy. It *is* the true and genuine secret to success in prayer—*the real thing!* When Peter and the disciples eagerly begged Jesus for bread, he did not give them a stone.

BUILDING ON A FIRM FOUNDATION

The disciples might have *wanted* a shortcut to experiencing what Jesus experienced when he prayed. But what Jesus gave them was far more. He gave them the tools to build their own "house" of prayer. He gave them the *foundation* for a personal relationship with God. He gave them the *basics* for the most important thing they—and we—would ever do: Talk with God.

Prayer is a beautiful foretaste of something we will experience for all eternity. Paradise lost will soon become paradise regained . . . and a whole lot more. For *we* will experience something not even Adam and Eve experienced—face-to-face communication with the very One who taught us the Prayer of Jesus.

And that *is* something to get excited about . . . grab hold of . . . and throw ourselves into heart and soul.

It really *is* the chance of a lifetime . . . and all eternity!

D28

You've been around the block a few times—though not nearly as many as some of us "older models." But still, you've probably collected a few dings and scratches of your own in the School of Hard Knocks. It's called "experience" . . . and it's how we learn to tell the difference between empty promises and the real thing. It *also* tells us what it takes to achieve what's worthwhile . . . *if* we're paying attention.

→ **Here's why I think people fall for "secrets of success":**

→ **I know the Prayer of Jesus is the "real thing" because**

→ **Here's what I'm going to have to do to make prayer really "work" in my life:**

DAY29

"For Yours Is the Kingdom . . ."

Yours, O Lᴏʀᴅ, is the greatness
and the power and the glory
and the majesty and the splendor,
for everything in heaven and earth is yours.
— 1 CHRONICLES 29:11 (ɴɪᴠ)

For yours is the kingdom and the power and the glory forever." With these closing words, the Prayer of Jesus comes full circle. In the end—as in the beginning—we praise and adore God's awesome majesty.

With these words, our thoughts move away from the things—and needs—of our earthly lives, *back* to heavenly things. Things like God's greatness, power, glory, majesty, and splendor.

With these words we express our faith in God's power . . . our trust in his loving care . . . and our hope of spending eternity in his presence.

They are words that lift our hearts and give *wings* to our spirits. And they are words that make the prayer truly "personal" . . . because they are the words Jesus left up to *us!*

PRAYING AS THE CHILDREN OF ISRAEL PRAYED

For centuries, the Jewish people ended their prayers with from-the-heart exclamations of praise for God's majesty, power, and glory.

No matter what the prayer was about—or how set in stone the "official" words—a prayer just didn't feel *complete* to them without that final, off-the-cuff, outburst of praise. So, at the end of *his* prayer pattern, Jesus left room for the way he knew *people* would pray.

D29

And that's exactly why so many English translations of the Bible include these extra words of praise—added by people over the centuries—at the end of the Prayer of Jesus.

ADDING THE PERSONAL TOUCH

Jesus could have "filled in the blanks" by providing an ending of his own, but he didn't. Because he wanted you to use your imagination! So he left room for your *personal* celebration of God's glory and power.

And he's not looking for canned "sound bites," either! What he wants are the thoughts—in your own words—that flow from deep within your heart and soul when you think about God.

In fact, *all* the parts and petitions of the Prayer of Jesus are meant to be launching pads for your personal thoughts and words for God. And when you come to the "end" of the prayer . . . you can keep right on going, just as long as you want to! Jesus left room. Because he knows how people are.

A VERY HUMAN THING TO DO . . .

Have you ever noticed how we humans have trouble "letting go" of special things? When something touches our hearts—or moves us deeply—we want to hang on to the moment.

Have you ever watched tears stream down the face of an Olympic gold medalist, as his country's flag is raised because of something *he* did? Have you ever witnessed an act of heroism or compassion that brought a lump to your throat? Or heard a glorious piece of music that made your heart soar?

Then you know what I mean. You don't want the moment to end. You want to be *part* of it.

The words of Jesus' perfect prayer must surely have moved the early Christians in that same way. They, too, must have wanted the moment to last "just a little longer"—and found their own words to say *again* what Jesus' words said to *them*. Just as you can!

Some things *are* just too good to let go of easily. And some things *do* bear repeating. What if *you* had been one of the early Christians . . . hearing the Prayer of Jesus for the very first time? How do you think it might have affected you? And how would it compare with other special "moments" in your life?

→ I remember *this* moment I didn't want to end:

→ If I were hearing the Prayer of Jesus for the very *first* time, I think it would make me feel

→ If I wanted to sum up what Jesus' prayer says, these are the words I would use:

DAY 30

"Amen."

> *The Amen is the One who*
> *is the faithful and true*
> *witness. He is the ruler*
> *of all that God has made.*
>
> — REVELATION 3:14 (ICB)

"Amen." Everyone knows the word. We tack it onto the end of every prayer. There's even a joyful, hand-clapping gospel song that is nothing *but* amens.

But have you ever stopped to think what it actually *means?* Probably not . . . or you'd be saying it much more thoughtfully.

"Amen," you see, is a lot *more* than just a handy way to sign off a prayer. It's *more* than saying, "That's all, God," . . . like a cartoon character ending a film with "Th-th-th-that's all, folks!" "Amen" is *agreeing* to the truth of God's holy Word. "Amen" is *pledging* to honor God's will!

When you add that simple, little, taken-for-granted word, what you are *really* saying is: "May things happen the way *you*—in your infinite wisdom—decide they should, Lord."

◼◻ NOT A SIGN-OFF . . . A SIGN-UP!

"Amen" is like writing your name in big, bold letters on the sign-up sheet for God's team—saying, "I want to be part of the wonders that happen when we work together."

"Amen" is carving your initials into the Tree of Life.

"Amen" is your personal signature on a love letter to God—telling him your prayer comes not just from your head . . . but from your heart.

THE MODEL OF PERFECTION

The most perfect example of amen-in-action is Jesus. In fact, in Revelation he is *called* "Amen, the faithful and true witness" . . . the One who testifies to God's truth and submits to God's will in all things.

Jesus stepped out of heaven to put on human flesh . . . and human frailty. He knew hunger and frustration and disappointment and temptation. He suffered and died . . . for us. Because it was God's will.

Nothing was too much to ask of him. Even when he knelt—alone and lonely—in the Garden of Gethsemane, he said "amen" to the suffering he knew was to come. Because *nothing* was more important than doing God's will.

HAVING THE LAST WORD

"Amen" traditionally comes at the end of prayer. But it is the *first* thing we should have in mind, because it is a marvelous reminder that the *purpose* of prayer is to bring us into harmony with God's will . . . and not the other way around!

When you place "Amen"—like a powerful punctuation mark—at the end of the Prayer of Jesus, you are not *finishing* anything. Rather, you are telling God, "I meant every word!"

You are letting God know you've got your F-A-C-T-S straight—that you will make Faith, Adoration, Confession, Thanksgiving, and Supplication a living part of who you are.

You are saying, "Do with me what you will, Lord. I'm in your hands."

And that's when the door opens. Because when you place yourself—with complete trust—in God's hands, you are not at the *end* of anything. You are standing at . . .

— THE *BEGINNING* —

D30

Who would have guessed that one little word could say so *much*? And now that you do know, how do you think it will affect the way you pray?

→ **It's true, I used to think "Amen" meant**

→ **Now I see the most important thing it says is**

→ **Here are some ways I can "test" the things I do, to see if they work with God's will:**

PRAYER TRACKER

After reflecting on the "Prayer of Jesus" as the **perfect** model for all your prayers, you may be asking, **"Now what?** How do I keep **growing** in this new relationship with my heavenly Father?"

Well, that's where the Prayer Tracker comes in. The forms on the next few pages are **designed** to help you create your own daily prayer journal. I encourage you to copy them and make a notebook to record your conversations with **God.** Get to know your heavenly Father and rely on him.

As you spend time alone with God in your secret place, the Prayer Tracker will help you remember that prayer is meant to be a **two-way** conversation—a special kind of **"music"** that you and God create *together.* And the more you practice, the more you *listen,* the more you bring yourself into harmony with God . . . the clearer the music becomes.

Use it every day. And . . . **ENJOY** the music!

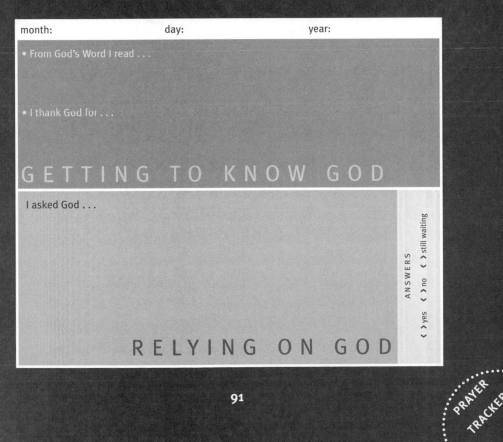

month: day: year:

• From God's Word I read . . .

• I thank God for . . .

GETTING TO KNOW GOD

I asked God . . .

ANSWERS   < > yes   < > no   < > still waiting

RELYING ON GOD

PRAYER TRACKER

PRAYER TRACKER

month: day: year:

- From God's Word I read . . .

- I thank God for . . .

GETTING TO KNOW GOD

I asked God . . .

ANSWERS
< > yes < > no < > still waiting

RELYING ON GOD

---

month: day: year:

- From God's Word I read . . .

- I thank God for . . .

GETTING TO KNOW GOD

I asked God . . .

ANSWERS
< > yes < > no < > still waiting

RELYING ON GOD

PRAYER TRACKER

month: day: year:

• From God's Word I read . . .

• I thank God for . . .

GETTING TO KNOW GOD

I asked God . . .

ANSWERS

< > yes   < > no   < > still waiting

RELYING ON GOD

---

month: day: year:

• From God's Word I read . . .

• I thank God for . . .

GETTING TO KNOW GOD

I asked God . . .

ANSWERS

< > yes   < > no   < > still waiting

RELYING ON GOD

PRAYER TRACKER

month: day: year:

• From God's Word I read . . .

• I thank God for . . .

GETTING TO KNOW GOD

I asked God . . .

ANSWERS ‹ › yes ‹ › no ‹ › still waiting

RELYING ON GOD

month: day: year:

• From God's Word I read . . .

• I thank God for . . .

GETTING TO KNOW GOD

I asked God . . .

ANSWERS ‹ › yes ‹ › no ‹ › still waiting

RELYING ON GOD

PRAYER TRACKER

month: day: year:

• From God's Word I read . . .

• I thank God for . . .

GETTING TO KNOW GOD

I asked God . . .

ANSWERS

‹ › yes ‹ › no ‹ › still waiting

RELYING ON GOD

---

month: day: year:

• From God's Word I read . . .

• I thank God for . . .

GETTING TO KNOW GOD

I asked God . . .

ANSWERS

‹ › yes ‹ › no ‹ › still waiting

RELYING ON GOD

PRAYER TRACKER

PRAYER TRACKER

month: day: year:

• From God's Word I read . . .

• I thank God for . . .

GETTING TO KNOW GOD

I asked God . . .

ANSWERS

< > yes   < > no   < > still waiting

RELYING ON GOD

month: day: year:

• From God's Word I read . . .

• I thank God for . . .

GETTING TO KNOW GOD

I asked God . . .

ANSWERS

< > yes   < > no   < > still waiting

RELYING ON GOD

PRAYER TRACKER

PRAYER TRACKER

month: day: year:

• From God's Word I read . . .

• I thank God for . . .

GETTING TO KNOW GOD

I asked God . . .

RELYING ON GOD

---

month: day: year:

• From God's Word I read . . .

• I thank God for . . .

GETTING TO KNOW GOD

I asked God . . .

RELYING ON GOD

PRAYER TRACKER

PRAYER TRACKER

month: day: year:

- From God's Word I read . . .

- I thank God for . . .

GETTING TO KNOW GOD

I asked God . . .

ANSWERS ⟨ ⟩ yes   ⟨ ⟩ no   ⟨ ⟩ still waiting

RELYING ON GOD

month: day: year:

- From God's Word I read . . .

- I thank God for . . .

GETTING TO KNOW GOD

I asked God . . .

ANSWERS ⟨ ⟩ yes   ⟨ ⟩ no   ⟨ ⟩ still waiting

RELYING ON GOD